Emily's Perfect Christmas Tree

By Catherine Christensen Illustrated by Jane Delve

To Dad, Mom, Emily, Daniel, and
Jessie for our wonderful years of
Christmas tree hunting.
—Catherine

To Ben, Eve, Joseph, and Matthew
for making my world magical.
—Jane

Emily's Perfect Christmas Tree

By Catherine Christensen · Illustrated By Jane Delve

Sweetwater Books · An Imprint of Cedar Fort, Inc. · Springville, Utah

ISBN 13: 978-1-4621-1750-5

Published by Sweetwater Books, an imprint of Cedar Fort, Inc.,
2373 W. 700 S., Springville, UT 84663
Distributed by Cedar Fort, Inc., www.cedarfort.com

LIBRARY OF CONGRESS CATALOGING-IN-PUBLICATION DATA

Christensen, Catherine, 1988- author.
  Emily's perfect Christmas tree / Catherine Christensen.
       pages cm
  Summary: Emily and her family go shopping for a Christmas tree, but when none of the trees fits her vision of a "perfect" tree, she worries that Christmas will not be perfect.
  ISBN 978-1-4621-1750-5 (hardback : alk. paper)
  1. Christmas stories. [1. Stories in rhyme. 2. Christmas--Fiction. 3. Christmas trees--Fiction. 4. Jesus Christ--Nativity--Fiction.] I. Title.
  PZ8.3.C4562Em 2015
  [E]--dc23
                          2015011175

Page design by Michelle May and Rebecca J. Greenwood
Cover design by Michelle May
Cover design © 2015 by Lyle Mortimer
Edited by Melissa J. Caldwell

Printed and bound in China

10 9 8 7 6 5 4 3 2 1

Printed on acid-free paper

Here's Whiskers, our little mouse friend. Looks like she scampered all over the book! Can you spot Whiskers thirteen times?

Emily and her family
Went to pick out their
Christmas tree.

Row upon row of trees stood tall—

Emily would inspect them all.

This year,
a single wish
had she:

To find the perfect Christmas tree!

That tree's too **fat**.

This tree's too *thin.*

That one looks like a *violin.*

"That tree's crooked.
This tree's b a r e."

Emily studied them with care.

Dad said, "This small one's rather nice.
And better yet, it's cheaply priced!"

"It's way too small," said Emily.
"I don't think that's the perfect tree."

"This tree is cute!
Its branches $curl$."
Mom smiled and
gave the tree a twirl.

"That green
is weird!" said Emily.

"I don't think that's
the perfect tree!"

"I like this one," her brother said
And grabbed a different tree instead.

"It's **bent** on top," said Emily.

"I don't think that's the **perfect tree.**"

They searched until
the family stopped
Beside the
last tree
on the lot.

"There's something wrong—it's not quite right.

Perhaps the shape?

Perhaps the height?"

"That's true," said Dad,
"I do agree.
But this will have
to be our tree."

"Let's look again?
We can't be done.

Maybe we
missed
the perfect one."

Mom sighed. "I'm sorry, Emily.
I doubt there IS a perfect tree."
Emily scowled as they drove back,
The tree tied to the
car's roof rack.

But soon her frown
began to fade,

As they hung ornaments
they'd made.

Gingerbread men and popcorn strings,
Cardboard angels with glued-on wings.
Emily gasped, "The tree looks great,

Sparkling, colorful,
tall, and straight."

Next they wrapped
up gifts with bows.

Emily tingled
to her toes!

They placed the gifts
beneath the tree,
Signs of love for her family.

"I was wrong!
This tree's not bad—
Maybe the best we've
ever had."

They sipped hot drinks and munched on treats
While snuggling close in cozy seats.
And in that circle round the tree,
Dad read of the Nativity:

The baby born
beneath the star,
Long ago in
a land afar.

Emily looked up with a grin.

"That star will help me
think of Him.

This tree's perfect!"
she said, surprised.

"Shape doesn't matter,
nor does size.

It helped us love
and have great fun.

It helped us think
about God's Son."

They stood within the
tree's soft glow,

And watched the
gently falling snow.

"My wish came true," said Emily. "We found the **perfect** Christmas tree."

Jane decided that she wanted to be an artist at the tender age of eight when she created a large painting of a chair, letting her creative juices flow! Studying the chair's "interesting" perspective, Jane's quick-witted yet kind teacher commented that it was as though he was gazing upon a Van Gogh. She took that as the greatest of encouragements and hasn't stopped painting since. She is an English girl living in Wales with her very patient husband and three children.

Catherine loves books. She reads books, writes books, edits books, collects books, and even shelved books at the library for her first job. She also loves to travel and explore the world with her husband, Jon, and her daughter, Juliette. Catherine earned her BA from Brigham Young University. She grew up in England and now lives in Springville, Utah.